RACHEL FRIEDMAN
Is Not the Queen

Also by Sarah Kapit

Rachel Friedman Breaks the Rules

Rachel Friedman and Eight Not-Perfect Nights of Hanukkah

Second Chance Summer

The Many Mysteries of the Finkel Family

Get a Grip, Vivy Cohen!

RACHEL FRIEDMAN IS NOT THE QUEEN

SARAH KAPIT

ILLUSTRATED BY GENEVIEVE KOTE

HENRY HOLT AND COMPANY
New York

Henry Holt and Company, *Publishers since 1866*
Henry Holt® is a registered trademark of Macmillan Publishing Group, LLC
120 Broadway, New York, NY 10271 • mackids.com

Text copyright © 2025 by Sarah Kapit. Illustrations copyright © 2025 by
Genevieve Kote. All rights reserved.

Our books may be purchased in bulk for promotional, educational, or business
use. Please contact your local bookseller or the Macmillan Corporate and
Premium Sales Department at (800) 221-7945 ext. 5442 or by email at
MacmillanSpecialMarkets@macmillan.com.

Library of Congress Cataloging-in-Publication Data is available.

First edition, 2025
Book design by Abby Granata
Printed in the United States of America by Lakeside Book Company,
Crawfordsville, Indiana

ISBN 978-1-250-88112-0 (hardcover)
1 3 5 7 9 10 8 6 4 2

ISBN 978-1-250-88110-6 (paperback)
1 3 5 7 9 10 8 6 4 2

To Jayne Carlin

CHAPTER 1
The Mission

I have a mission, and it is so important. The most important!

I, Rachel Friedman, am a knight. And I am going to save the princess. Who also happens to be my cat, Cookie. Right now, Cookie is trapped in the dungeon—well, the laundry room—and I am the only one who can save her! My best friend, Maya, is here to be my assistant.

"I'm coming for you, Princess Cookie!" I say in a loud voice. (Knights are loud. It's just part of their thing.)

I wave my plastic sword for dramatic effect. In fact, I wave it so dramatically that I hit Maya by accident.

"Ow! *Rach-el*, you hit me," Maya complains.

I flinch. Really, I didn't mean to hurt my bestest friend in the entire world.

"So sorry, dear Knight Maya. Can you continue on our quest, or do you need to stop for a Band-Aid?"

"It wasn't that bad," Maya says. "I'm just saying you should be more careful, okay?"

"Yeah, okay."

I turn to Maya and grin. "Let's go!"

We burst through the door to the laundry room. Mountains of clothes are everywhere. I guess my dad hasn't done the laundry yet. I pretend the hampers are piles of lava rocks in a dark and dangerous dungeon. Do dungeons have lava? They should.

"Princess Cookie, where are you? I am here to rescue you!" I call out.

"Rachel, I don't think she's here," Maya says.

"She must be," I insist.

But after several minutes of looking, I have to admit that Maya is right. Cookie is nowhere to be found in the laundry room. She's not in any of the hampers, or the cupboard, or even the washer and dryer machines.

"I fear we are too late. The princess must have escaped on her own," I say.

We trudge back upstairs. Sure enough, Cookie is sitting in her usual spot by the window, purring loudly. She is still wearing the cloth crown I made for her.

"You were supposed to wait for the

knights to come and rescue you!" I scold her. "But good job on the escape."

I turn to Maya. "What do we do now, Knight Maya?"

She takes off her knight helmet and smiles. "Maybe now we can play princesses!"

I make a face. Princesses isn't my favorite game. "Can't we do another round of knights?"

Maya crosses her arms over her chest. "We just did knights!"

"I know, but we didn't get to finish everything the right way."

I don't know why Maya's being weird. I thought she liked playing knights just as much as I do. But now she's shaking her head at me.

"Why do we always have to do what you

want to do, Rachel? I want to play princesses!"

"But princesses are boring. All they do is sit there," I protest.

"They do not!"

I open my mouth, ready to argue back. I have so many good ideas in my head about how knights are obviously better than princesses. I am sure that I can convince Maya. But before I can say anything else, Dad enters the room. He clears his throat.

"Time for dinner, girls!" he announces.

We both run to the kitchen before he even finishes his sentence.

I still feel a little weird about things, though. Usually Maya and I agree on everything.

I don't like this feeling.

CHAPTER 2

Meant for a Crown

I feel better after eating grilled cheese. Grilled cheese always makes everything better, in my opinion.

While we eat, Dad does that thing he does when he asks Maya and me a bunch of questions. I love my dad, but he asks way too many questions.

"So, how's Hebrew school going?" he asks.

That's another thing about Dad. Sometimes—a lot of the time—he asks about the most boring things ever. I mean, Hebrew school?! Who wants to talk about Hebrew school?

I shrug. "The same. So. Boring!"

Dad shakes his head and smiles at me. "And what about you, Maya? Do you agree with Rachel on this one?"

Maya finishes chewing before she answers.

"Yeah. Hebrew school is . . . Hebrew school." But then she breaks into a wide grin. "But Purim is going to be super fun this year! I can't wait."

"That's right," Dad says. "The third graders put on the Purim spiel, don't they?"

"Yep!" Maya says.

Now that Dad and Maya mention it, I *am* pretty excited about Purim coming up. Purim just so happens to be my second-favorite Jewish holiday. (My very favorite is Hanukkah, because of the presents. Duh. But Purim is pretty great, too.)

Some people say that Purim is like the Jewish Halloween—which is another one of my favorite holidays! We don't go trick-or-treating, but everyone dresses up in costumes. There's this awesome carnival at the synagogue with games and everything. And this year, I'm going to do something even more special. Every year, all the third graders get to be in the Purim spiel. The Purim spiel is a play about the story of Purim. We're going to perform in front of the whole congregation!

I have been waiting *forever* to be in the Purim spiel.

"I am going to be Queen Esther! It's going to be the best," I announce.

Queen Esther is the most important character in the whole story. She's the one who saved everyone! She's like a superhero, only cooler. And she gets to wear a crown.

I look to Maya for support. She agrees with me. Right? But her eyes are pointed away. So weird.

Just as I'm trying to figure out what's up with Maya, Dad looks at me with a frown. "Did your teacher already tell you that you're going to be Queen Esther, Rachel?"

I squirm in my chair, just a little bit. "Well, no. But I *want* to be her!"

Dad's face still looks very serious. I do not like his serious face very much at all. He squeezes me on the shoulder.

"It's good to have ambitions. But we don't always get everything we want."

I guess he's right. But still. I want to be Queen Esther. And I think I'm going to be Queen Esther.

If you ask me, I'm just meant to be a queen.

CHAPTER 3
The Story of Esther plus Some Other People

I make a face at my Hebrew workbook. For the past bazillion minutes—okay, half hour—I've been working on a reading exercise. I'm supposed to be learning about Hebrew vowels. Which isn't a very

interesting topic in my opinion. I'm not good at remembering what all the dots and squiggles are supposed to mean. Someone should fix that, in my opinion.

"And we are done with reading for the day!" Ms. Rosenberg says.

Finally! Reading is definitely my least favorite part about Hebrew school. I close my workbook with a nice loud smack. I grin at Maya. She's sitting next to me, like always.

"It's time to talk about Purim," Ms. Rosenberg says.

Ooh, yes! This is what I have been waiting for.

"This year, we have a very important responsibility," Ms. Rosenberg explains. "We will be acting out the Purim spiel for the entire congregation. Can someone remind us what the Purim spiel is?"

"It's the story of Purim!"

I blurt out my answer without raising my hand first. Whoops. I know I'm not supposed to do that, but sometimes I just can't help myself.

Ms. Rosenberg smiles at me. "That's right. So, to start off, let's review the story of Purim."

I play with my pen while Ms. Rosenberg goes over the story. Even though I'm super excited about the Purim spiel, I don't understand why we have to talk about this *again*. I already know the story! I bet I could teach the class myself.

Here's how the story goes.

THE STORY OF PURIM (BY ME):

A really long time ago, a bunch of people lived in the kingdom of Persia. There was a king who ruled over everything, and his name was Achashverosh. Which is a really, really long name. People must have wasted a lot of time just saying his name and stuff.

Anyway, King Long-Name was married to Queen Vashti. He ordered Queen Vashti around. That's not a very nice thing to do, ever. Girls should be able to do whatever they want! And Queen Vashti didn't do everything the king wanted her to do, so he took away her crown. Again—not a very nice thing to do!

So then the king needed a new queen.

He chose Esther. Queen Esther was Jewish, but she didn't tell the king. Her cousin Mordechai told Esther that she shouldn't tell the king about being Jewish. (Personally, I think this king sounds like a real jerk. Jewish people should be able to tell other people that we're Jewish! That is just basic.)

Mordechai sat around the gate to the king's palace a lot. Which is kind of weird. Didn't he have anything better to do? But one day, it paid off! Mordechai overheard two guys plotting to kill the king. Mordechai told Esther about it, and Esther told the king. So King Long-Name didn't die, and from then on the king really liked Mordechai. Because duh!

But the king still wasn't the best person in the world. He had an adviser named Haman, and Haman was plain evil. Haman went around the streets and asked everyone to bow down to him. Rude! Who did this Haman think he was, anyway? Mordechai wouldn't bow down to Haman because Jews don't do that kind of thing. And then Haman got really, really mad.

Haman found out that Mordechai was Jewish. He decided that he wanted to kill all Jews in the kingdom. (Total overreaction! Seriously.) Haman convinced the king to go along with his evil plan. Even more proof that King Long-Name kind of stunk as a person. Or at least he wasn't very good at standing up to people, which is pretty weird for a king.

Luckily, Mordechai found out about Haman's evil plan. I guess he was smart like that. Mordechai told Esther what Haman was going to do. Then Esther finally told the king that she was Jewish, and she asked the king to, you know, not kill all Jewish people. King Long-Name decided to call off Haman's plan. It kind of seems like the very least he could do. Still. Esther and Mordechai were really brave, and now every year we celebrate their bravery.

So, that's the story. And this year, we are going to perform it!

I raise my hand. (See, sometimes I can remember to do that.)

"Yes, Rachel?" Ms. Rosenberg asks.

"I want to be Queen Esther!" I say. Telling people what I want usually works out for me. Like when I tell Dad what I want for Hanukkah!

Ms. Rosenberg smiles at me, but it's kind of a weird smile. I frown. I don't like it when adults smile like that.

"I'll keep that in mind, but we're going to have auditions for all the parts next Sunday," she says. "Everyone has an equal chance at being Queen Esther or Mordechai or any other part."

Okay, I guess that makes sense.

But I still really, really want to be Esther.

CHAPTER 4

Queens of Purim

I'm still bouncing with excitement when Dad picks Maya and me up from Hebrew school.

"We're doing the Purim spiel! And I'm going to be the queen!" I tell him.

Maya frowns. "That's not what Ms. Rosenberg said, Rachel."

"Okay, okay. You're right. But I want to be Queen Esther." I look at Maya. "What about you? What part do you want?"

I really should have thought about this sooner. After all, Maya is my best friend! She needs to have a really great part in the Purim spiel, too.

Maya bites her lip. "I . . . I don't know."

Well, that's okay! I can help her out.

"Maybe you can be Mordechai," I suggest. "Ms. Rosenberg said that girls can play boy parts and the other way around."

I expect Maya to like that idea, but she only bites her lip again and shrugs.

"Maybe. I just want an important part, but . . ."

"But what?" I ask.

She looks down at her hands.

"I'll probably just be a tree or something."

I poke her shoulder. "Don't be silly! You're going to be a star with me."

I expect her to smile. She doesn't.

"Maybe," she mumbles.

I don't understand why she's being so weird. Maybe Maya is scared about performing in front of everyone. She can be a little shy sometimes. Before our first gymnastics competition, Maya got so nervous that she threw up. (I was sitting right next to her, so I definitely won't be forgetting that. Yuck!)

So I guess it makes sense that she's a little scared now, too. Well, that's okay. I'll do my best to help Maya. Because that is what best friends do.

For the first time ever, I am excited about Hebrew school when Sunday comes around again. Today's the day! Ms. Rosenberg is going to tell us which parts we're going to play in the Purim spiel.

First, we're going to read from the script she gave us. This is called an audition, and I've been practicing for it all week. Maybe I'm not always the best at remembering every single line, but Dad says I am very dramatic in saying them. (My brother Aaron made a joke about how I'm always dramatic. Like he's one to talk!)

Anyway. I do a pretty good job during my audition. Ms. Rosenberg says so! I know that I'm going to be Queen Esther.

Maya looks really nervous before her audition, so I squeeze her shoulder.

"Good luck," I tell her.

"Thanks, Rachel."

But she still looks like she might fall over at any second.

Waiting for everyone to finish their auditions takes a really, really long time. But finally it's done, and Ms. Rosenberg announces her decisions.

"In the role of Mordechai, we have Ethan. Ben is going to be King Achashverosh, and Ava will be Haman!"

Everyone claps at the announcement. I do, too, but to be honest I'm getting antsy. When is Ms. Rosenberg going to announce Esther? She's only the most important person in the story!

Ms. Rosenberg talks some more. This super-annoying girl Violet is going to be the narrator, and other kids are going to have small parts, like being a royal messenger. But I still don't hear my name. Or Maya's.

"And now, for our two queens! Rachel will be playing Queen Vashti, and Maya is going to be our Queen Esther. Mazel tov, everyone!"

I stare at Ms. Rosenberg. Did she just say what I think she said?

Next to me, Maya smiles her very biggest smile. She doesn't look nervous and sick anymore. And all of a sudden, everything feels wrong. I feel like there's an itch beneath my skin that I can't quite scratch. It's the same thing I felt when Maya got tickets to see a superspecial gymnastics show and I didn't.

For a few moments, I'm not sure what it is. But then I know. I'm jealous.

CHAPTER 5
The Fight

Ms. Rosenberg lets us have free time for the rest of Hebrew school, since everyone is way too excited to learn anyway. Normally, this would be the best thing ever. But I can't even enjoy free time right now. I'm too busy thinking about what just happened.

Why, oh *why*, did Ms. Rosenberg decide that I don't get to be Queen Esther? Am I not good enough? I know I'm not always the best at memorizing stuff, but ... I tried. I really, really tried.

I wanted so much to be Esther. I thought I would be Esther. And now I'm not.

To be honest, I don't want to be here right now. I want to go home and eat junk food and cuddle with Cookie while watching TV. That's my thing when life gets hard. But I have to stay. With Maya. Who is as excited as I've ever seen her.

"I can't believe it!" Maya keeps saying. "I just wanted to say more than one line. I had no idea I'd get to be the queen!"

"One of the queens," I say, because I just can't help myself. I mean, Vashti is also a queen. (The less important queen. But still.)

Maya waves a hand. "Right. But... *Esther*!"

"Mm-hmm," I say.

At that, Maya turns around and scowls at me. "You know, Rachel, you could at least pretend to be happy for me."

What? I cannot believe she is accusing me of not being happy for her. I am! I totally, totally am. Even though I'm maybe also sad for me. Is that so wrong, really?

"I am happy for you," I tell her.

"Well, you're not acting like it."

I cross my arms over my chest. "What do you want me to do? Jump up and down for you? Make you a cupcake and throw a party?"

Maya glares at me and grinds her teeth.

"You could not do *that*," she says.

"Not do what?" I ask.

"Be mean!"

"I'm not . . . I'm not *being mean*," I protest.

"Well, you're definitely not acting like a good friend."

"I don't know what you want from me! Congratulations, okay? Does that make you happy?!"

Now Maya looks the furthest thing from happy.

"Whatever," she says.

I squirm.

CHAPTER 6

A Queen Stands Up for Herself

Maya and I don't talk for the rest of Hebrew school or the ride home. When Dad asks us questions, I talk to him, but I keep my answers as short as I can.

For once in my life, I am not in the mood for talking. Even when Dad drops Maya off, I'm still not in the mood.

"So," Dad says while Maya skips to the front door of her house. "You're going to be Queen Vashti, huh? So exciting!"

"Not really," I say before I can help myself.

My brother snorts from the front seat. I thought he was reading a book, but I guess he's been listening after all. Typical annoying Aaron!

Dad ignores Aaron completely, which is the right thing to do. "I'm happy for you, sweetie. I'm sure you'll do a wonderful job in the play."

Aaron snorts again, and this time I can't ignore him. Even though he can't see me, I scowl.

"Aaa-ron, just say whatever you're going to say. And stop snorting. You sound like a walrus with the flu."

"How would you know what a walrus with the flu sounds like?" Aaron asks.

"It's called using your imagination! Anyway. You obviously want to say something to me. About Purim."

"Oh, it's nothing," Aaron says. But I can tell from the way he's talking that it is something. "I was just thinking about how Vashti is the perfect part for you."

That just makes me scowl even more. It's not like Aaron knows what he's talking about. Of course he doesn't. But still. Why would he say that Vashti is the perfect part for me when I am *obviously* meant to be Esther? He's just like Ms. Rosenberg!

Besides, when Aaron was in the Purim spiel, he played Mordechai. That's the second-most important character in the play! He couldn't possibly understand how I feel right now. But I guess he just has to rub it in. So annoying!

"What makes you say that?" I ask Aaron. Really, someone should congratulate me for how nice I'm being to him.

Even though all I can see of Aaron is the back of his head, I can just imagine him smirking.

"Oh, well, it's just that Vashti was very

stubborn, right? She wouldn't listen to anyone, not even the king. That sounds a lot like you, Rachel."

I have to admit that he has a point. And I always did like that Vashti wouldn't let anyone else push her around. But that doesn't mean I want to be her in the play.

"Yeah, sure," I say. "Vashti stood up for herself, and that's cool. But she stood up for herself so much that she's out of the

play in the first five minutes! How boring is that?"

"On the plus side, at least you won't have to memorize many lines," Aaron says.

That is such an annoying thing to say. It's like Aaron thinks I can't memorize lines. I totally can. Ugh, I bet he's smirking again. My brother is such a jerk!

"Whatever," I mumble. "It doesn't matter. I don't care."

Except that I do.

CHAPTER 7
A Challenging Challenge

My dad loves to say that a good night's sleep makes everything better. Usually he's right about this stuff, but not now. When I wake up the next day, I still feel bad about the Purim spiel.

I just don't understand why Ms. Rosenberg thinks I can't play Esther. Am I not good enough? I know I'm not always the best at remembering lines and stuff. It's just hard for me to concentrate a lot of the time, even with my ADHD medicine. There's just so much going on and I have so many thoughts and feelings and . . . and sometimes I forget which Hebrew letter makes the "shh" sound and which one is the regular "s." That stuff is hard!

Is that why she gave me a part with almost no lines? Because she thinks I won't be able to remember what to say?

But I try to put all that aside, because today is a good day. For some reason, I don't have to go to school! And this afternoon I get to do my very favorite thing in the whole entire world: gymnastics practice! Unlike with Hebrew school things, I am actually good at gymnastics. I was the very first girl in my class to learn how to do a perfect front tuck. Not that it's a competition or anything. (It totally is a competition.)

I arrive at the gym wearing the purple leotard Dad bought me for Hanukkah, just for extra luck.

When I get to the main part of the gym, I see Maya. It's the first time I've seen her since the whole Queen Esther thing. She's

stretching out her legs on the mats. Normally I would run up to her so we can be together . . . but I don't. Not today.

I look at her. Maya looks back at me. I can't tell what she's thinking.

Probably she's still mad at me. So I go find a mat on the other side of the room. I start doing my warm-up stretches by myself. (Stretching is not the most fun part of gymnastics, but Coach Kayla says that it is very important.)

Soon, Coach Kayla calls the class to the center of the gym. "Today we're going to do a very special challenge," she says.

Right away, I perk up. I love Coach Kayla's special challenges. That's what she calls her special exercises to help us improve our gymnastics skills. Sometimes the challenges are a little silly, but they are always, *always* fun.

"Let's get moving over to the beam!" Coach Kayla says, still using her Excited Voice.

But now I am not excited. The balance beam is my least favorite event. It's just not my thing. Why did the challenge have to involve the beam? I have no luck at all!

Also . . . beam is Maya's best event. She's probably going to beat me—again.

Even though I am very, very not-happy, I try to pay attention while Coach Kayla explains the challenge. We're all going to be standing up on the beam with one leg in the air. Whoever stays on the beam for the longest amount of time wins.

"This is going to be harder than it looks," my coach warns. "You'll need to use all your beam skills and really concentrate."

She doesn't have to tell me that it's going to be hard. I already know that, thank you very much.

Of course, that will make it even better when I win. Because I *have* to win.

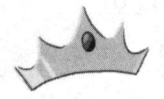

CHAPTER 8
The Balance Beam Queen

Before I jump onto the beam, I take a deep breath. Coach Kayla is big on taking deep breaths, and usually it helps. I can totally, *totally* do this.

Except . . . I feel wobbly the moment my feet touch the beam. Which is really, really not good. Focus, Rachel! Focus on the beam.

I feel kind of weird standing up here with a bunch of other girls, but I try to forget about them. Distractions just get in the way.

I lift up my left leg. Maybe I'm not the most graceful, but that's okay. The point of the challenge isn't to be graceful.

Of course I notice Maya standing on the other end of the beam. She still is my best friend, after all, and best friends look out for each other. Maya totally looks like a ballerina with one leg stretched out behind her. I know that she's going to win this challenge.

No! I need to win.

"Good job!" Coach Kayla calls from her place on the mat. "Keep it up."

I grind my teeth. I'm feeling pretty shaky, and I'd really just like to jump off the beam entirely. But I can't. I won't.

One by one, the other girls slip up. They fall onto the mat. Soon it's only me and Maya on the beam.

One of us is going to win, and the other one is going to lose.

I look over at her. She isn't smiling. In fact, her mouth is set into a firm line. She wants to win this just as much as I do. I know it.

That doesn't matter, though. It's going to be me.

"Getting tired?" I call over to Maya.

She scowls. "Distracting me isn't going to work, Rachel."

"I'm not trying to distract you. I'm just talking. Don't you want to talk with me?"

At that she scowls even more. "Now you want to talk? That's new. Fifteen minutes ago you couldn't get away from me fast enough."

Even though I'm keeping my balance, my stomach does a little flip-flop. I guess Maya noticed that I didn't come up to her

earlier, when we were doing warm-ups. I feel bad about that now, but I'm not going to let her know that. I just give her a big Rachel smile. Maybe it's a little bit fake. But still. I'm smiling!

Right when I'm coming up with something else to say, I topple over onto the mat.

"Blech! No, no, no," I say.

I've fallen off the beam loads of times before. Obviously. But I really, really wanted to stay on today. I wanted to beat Maya.

The fall doesn't hurt that much, really. But also, it does.

"Looks like Maya is our balance beam champion," Coach Kayla says. "You showed a lot of skill and determination. Great job!"

Coach Kayla talks more, but I'm not really listening. All I can think about is how I lost to Maya. Again.

I don't speak for the rest of practice.

CHAPTER 9
Worse and Worser

For the rest of the week, everything keeps on being not-good. I miss Maya, even though I'm mad at her. I miss playing games with her during recess and hanging out together after school. Every day, she's been eating lunch with girls who are not me. I sit on the other end of the cafeteria, where I don't have to see her that much.

By the time Sunday comes around again, my mood is worse than ever. I don't want to go to Hebrew school and practice for the Purim spiel. There's no point to it. I have three lines! And one of those lines is just the word *no*.

I try to explain all of this to Dad, but he won't listen to me.

"You made a commitment, Rachel," he says. "You don't get to back out of it just because you didn't get exactly what you wanted."

"That's not why I don't want to go! I'm ... not feeling very well. I think I might throw up or something."

I'm not sick, really. But I let my voice shake a little for dramatic effect.

Dad frowns at me. He looks Very Worried.

"If you're feeling sick, of course you

don't have to go, hon. Do you need some medicine? Maybe the pink medicine—I know how much that helps you when you're having tummy problems. And should we make an appointment with Dr. Singh? I'm sure she can fit you in today."

I make a face. Maybe I don't want to be Vashti. But I definitely don't want to swallow the gross pink medicine and go to the doctor's office. Blech!

"I guess I'm okay," I mumble.

Dad smiles. "That's what I thought."

I try to Be Positive like Dad always tells me. I haven't seen Maya since Friday, which is practically forever ago. Maybe she's decided she isn't mad at me anymore. After all, we've had fights before. We've always made up. Sometimes we can't even remember why we started fighting in the first place. I just need to hope.

One of Maya's moms picks me up for Hebrew school, like usual. Normally Maya and I would talk the entire way there, but this time we don't. I think about it. I want to show Maya this funny cat video I found last night. But she obviously doesn't want to talk with me.

So much for hoping.

When we arrive at Ms. Rosenberg's room, I go to my usual seat. But Maya doesn't sit next to me. Instead, she walks over to the other side of the room next to Violet and her friends. Even though we both agree that Violet is super annoying. She's always bragging about going to Paris on vacation and blah, blah, blah.

Does Maya really like Violet better than me now?

For the first part of class, Ms. Rosenberg makes us do reading drills. I have even more trouble concentrating than usual. How am I supposed to think about Hebrew when my best friend in the whole entire world hates me?

Reading Hebrew is so bad that I actually feel happy when Ms. Rosenberg announces that it's Purim spiel time.

"If everyone can help move the desks, we can make a stage!" Ms. Rosenberg says.

Before I can even think about it, I run over to Maya. She's starting to push a desk to the back of the room. Even though Maya is doing okay, I decide to help her. I want to show that I can be a good best friend. (Or at least a better best friend than Violet.)

"Hi, Maya!" I say in my nicest voice. Maybe if I decide to be very, very nice to her, Maya will decide not to be mad at me anymore, and we can be best friends again.

"Hi, Rachel," she says.

But Maya doesn't sound happy to see me at all. She won't even look at me!

"Why are you still mad at me? Can't we just . . . forget about everything and start over?"

Now Maya looks at my face. *Finally*.

"Are you seriously even asking that question?" she says.

"Um, yes?"

Her eyes narrow and her lips become set in a thin line.

"First, you weren't happy for me when I got to be Esther. And then you totally ignored me at gymnastics class. *And then* you moped some more when I beat you at the competition. So, yes, Rachel. I'm still mad at you. No, we can't just forget about everything."

I drop my half of the desk. It falls to the floor with a loud thud. I should focus on that, but I can't. I'm too upset.

What she's saying makes sense. But it still really, really hurts.

"But . . . but I've tried to be nice today. I'm still . . . would you really rather hang out with *Violet* than me?!"

I don't mean to talk that loudly. Really, I don't. But I guess I talk too loud anyway. Loud enough for Violet to hear me. Whoops. I didn't realize she was so close. (Rude!)

Violet glares at me. She marches over with a very not-happy look on her face.

"That was really mean. See, Rachel, this

is why no one wants to be friends with you," she says.

My face gets so hot I'm afraid that I'll explode.

"That's not true!" I protest. "Lots of people want to be my friend."

Even after everything, some part of me still hopes that Maya will back me up like she always does. To say that we're still best friends, even after everything.

She doesn't.

As I turn away from them, I blink back tears.

CHAPTER 10
Not Enough Oomph

I am not, not, *not* in the mood to rehearse anything. But we're rehearsing anyway. Because I have no luck at all, we're starting the play from the very beginning. That's the only part where I have any lines.

Violet is the narrator, so she stands off to the side and explains what's going on. It's the perfect part for her since she loves to talk so much. (At least she gets a lot of lines. Unlike me. Not fair!)

"A long, long time ago, in the kingdom of Persia . . . ," she begins.

I tune her out almost as soon as she begins. Boring! This whole thing is boring. I hop from one foot to the other, just so I have something to do.

Other people start talking and I know I should pay attention, but I don't care about any of it. The king is acting all mean and stuff, blah, blah, blah. Everyone knows the story already. Why do we bother acting it out every single year?

Then I hear my name.

"Rachel!" Ms. Rosenberg says. "Rachel, are you paying attention?"

I snap back to the play.

"I'm paying attention," I lie. "What?"

Ms. Rosenberg smiles at me. "Rachel, you missed your first line."

My face heats up to a bazillion degrees. I only have a few lines, but somehow I've already messed up. This is the most embarrassing thing that has happened to me, ever.

"Right," I mumble. "Um . . . um . . ."

I know the line. I do, but I can't remember it. So I look down at my script and read.

"I am not doing what you tell me just because you're the king."

I know I should put more *oomph* behind the line, and normally I would totally do that. But I'm just not in the mood. At all.

"Vashti, why do you have to be so stubborn? Just come to the party with me. I need my wife to dance for the guests," Ben says in a great booming voice. I'd never guess that he's usually kind of quiet.

"NO!" I say.

At least I remembered that line without having to look at the script.

Ben goes through his next line, and I respond to him. And then Vashti leaves the play for good. Yay me.

I plop down on the floor along with everyone else who doesn't have a big part. Even though I'd rather do literally anything else, I watch the rest of the rehearsal.

Maya makes her big entrance.

"I don't know," Maya says to Ethan, the

boy playing Mordechai. "Shouldn't I tell the king I'm Jewish?"

Her voice shakes. Like she really is Queen Esther trying to figure out what to do.

I frown, just a little bit. Maya is good. Really, really good. She hardly has to look at her script at all. Not like me. Plus, she just *looks* like Esther. Sweet but also strong.

That's why I like her so much.

Still, I had no idea that she could *act*. Weird!

Maya and I have been best friends forever, but there's still so much I don't know about her.

I don't like it one bit.

CHAPTER 11
Going Off-Script

". . . And then everyone was happy in the kingdom of Shushan," Violet says.

That's the end of the play. Everyone claps, even me.

Ms. Rosenberg tells us that was a "good start." I think that means we still have a whole lot of work to do.

I really, really want to just go home

already, but Hebrew school doesn't get out for another thirty minutes. Blech.

"Let's take it from the top, actors," Ms. Rosenberg says.

So, we're going to start the play all over again.

I make a face and sigh. But even though I don't want to be here, I need to do better this time. Vashti may be a small, not-important part, but I still want to be the best Vashti ever.

This time, I try my hardest to pay attention when the play begins. Even to the really boring parts where Violet just reads lines.

Soon, it's my turn.

"I am not doing what you tell me just because you're the king!" I say. This time, I definitely do put some *oomph* into it. Out of

the corner of my eye, I can see Ms. Rosenberg smile.

Next, Ethan orders me to dance at the party. He glares at me in a way that looks real.

"NO!" I say.

That's the end of the line, and I know it. But while Ethan was talking and stomping around, I got an idea. A really good idea! Maybe Vashti has more to say.

"I will not listen to you, tyrant!" I say.

"Hold up!"

Ms. Rosenberg raises a hand. That's her signal to stop. She turns toward me.

"Rachel, that line isn't in the script."

I bounce on my feet. "I know. I just thought it might be more exciting?"

Still bouncing around, I wait for Ms. Rosenberg to answer. I know I probably should have just said the line from the script. It's just that I wanted to do *more*. Adding in a new line seemed like a good idea at the time.

She's going to tell me no. I'm sure of it.

Only she doesn't.

"We can add that line in," Ms. Rosenberg says. "It's a good one. But next time, ask before you go off-script. Okay, Rachel?"

I squeal. My idea worked! Now I have more lines.

Of course, I'm still out of the play in three minutes.

CHAPTER 12
A Difficult Question

I should be happy once Hebrew school is finally over for the day. I'm not. It's not like I actually want to stay longer or anything, but now I have to spend more time with Maya because Dad is driving us home.

She's probably still mad at me.

Ms. Rosenberg tells us we can leave, but I don't go over to Maya like I normally do. Instead, I take my time putting all my stuff in my backpack. Soon, I'm the only one left in the room.

"Rachel!" Ms. Rosenberg says. "I'm glad I have the chance to talk with you."

Uh-oh. If I know one thing, it's this: When teachers want to talk, it is *never* a good thing.

I smile anyway.

"Okay. We can talk."

"Great." She smiles back at me. "I wanted to check in to see if you're doing all right. You seemed to struggle at the beginning of rehearsal."

I fidget with my hands and stare down at the floor.

"I . . . I was just distracted." My voice is much more quiet than normal. "I did better the second time, right?"

Ms. Rosenberg nods.

"You did. I've just been wondering if there's anything that's upsetting you, Rachel. You haven't been yourself this past week."

Ugh, why do grown-ups always want to talk about feelings and stuff? I'd rather just *not*. But still, I kind of do have a question for her, and now is the perfect time for me to ask.

"Why didn't I get to be Queen Esther?" I blurt out.

The lines on Ms. Rosenberg's forehead get squiggly.

"That's a difficult question, Rachel," she says.

I make a face. Really, I shouldn't have even bothered trying to ask. It's not like she'd ever tell me the truth.

"Forget about it," I say.

"Wait, Rachel . . ."

But I'm already scurrying away.

Ten minutes later, I'm sitting in the back seat of Dad's car with Maya, again. We're not talking, again.

I glance over at her. I kind of want to say

something. The problem is, I have no idea what I can possibly say to make everything better. Anyway, Maya is reading a book, and I know she hates it when people interrupt her while she's reading.

At least Aaron isn't here to make things even worse. He went home to hang out with one of his friends. It must be nice, having friends.

When Dad finally pulls up to Maya's house, it's a ginormous relief.

Dad coughs as Maya starts getting out of the car.

"Rachel, aren't you going to say goodbye to Maya?"

I stare at my hands and frown.

"Bye, Maya," I say in a not-happy voice.

"Bye, Rachel," Maya says in a voice that is even more not-happy.

I look away while Maya starts walking

toward the front door to her house. But I can't escape Dad. He turns around to look at me and frowns.

"Rachel, is there something going on with you and Maya?"

I start playing with the strap to my seatbelt. "Um, kind of? We're fighting, kind of?"

"Hmm." Dad turns back to the wheel of

the car and starts driving toward our house. Since we're exactly five doors away from Maya's place, it's not a very long ride. "Do you want to talk about what's happening?"

I scowl.

"No, I don't."

CHAPTER 13
The Gifts of Purim

For the first time ever, I cannot wait for Purim to be over. I just want things to go back to the way they were before the stupid Purim spiel. Maybe once everything is done, Maya and I can go back to being friends. At least I can stop worrying about my lines.

Since I'm not hanging out with Maya

at all, I have plenty of time to practice my part. Even though I'm only going to be in the play for five minutes, I am going to make those five minutes count. No one will forget me!

I like to practice reading lines with Cookie. She plays the part of the king very well. To get into the spirit of the play, I give Cookie her toy crown. It's made out of cloth and has catnip inside. That keeps her busy while I practice.

Today, I am extra serious about practicing my lines. The play is tomorrow.

"I will not listen to you, tyrant!" I say to Cookie.

I frown. I need to put more feeling into it.

"I will not listen to you, tyrant!" I say, louder this time.

Cookie meows in response. I smile at her.

I read my lines a few more times, but I get bored with it pretty quickly. There are only so many times I can say the word *no*!

Well, okay. I've practiced as much as I possibly can.

Besides, it doesn't even matter. My part is so small that I might as well not even be there at all.

I sigh. Right now, I need a distraction. Luckily, I know just the thing.

"Come on," I say to Cookie. "You and me are both getting treats."

Cookie perks up at the sound of the word *treats*, and she races out into the kitchen ahead of me. I give her a treat first because she deserves it. Then I get some potato chips for myself and start munching on them.

"Rachey-bear!" Dad walks into the kitchen carrying a bunch of bags. "Just the girl I was looking for."

When Dad says that, it usually means he wants me to do something. Probably something super boring. But I'm already bored, so I don't really mind.

"What do I have to do now?" I ask in between potato chips.

Dad ruffles my hair.

"You don't *have* to do anything. But I would *like* for you to help me put together these mishloach manot."

I pop another potato chip into my mouth.

"The mish what?"

Dad laughs. "The Purim gift baskets! I was super on the ball this year, and I've bought enough treats for your entire Hebrew school class and Aaron's. I thought we'd have fun with it."

Now I remember all about mishloach manot. Jewish holidays have a lot of traditions, and one Purim tradition is to give gifts to other people. We don't remember to do it every year, but Dad likes making gift bags when we can. He's already gotten a bunch of bags that say HAPPY PURIM in bright colors.

I wish I was in a happy-Purim kind of mood. But I guess there are worse things to do than give gifts to other people. (Even though I like getting gifts more.)

And also . . . Dad will probably make me

give gifts to *everyone* in my Hebrew school class. Even Violet. Even Maya.

I gulp.

"Shouldn't Aaron have to do this, too?" I ask.

Because, really! It's only fair.

"Right you are, Rachey," Dad says with a smile. He heads to the living room to fetch Aaron. "Aaron Friedman, your presence is required!"

When Aaron comes in, he's pretty grumpy.

"Dad, come on. I was about to finish the game."

But Dad just gives another one of his Dad smiles.

"You'll finish the game after you're done helping us with the gift bags."

Aaron still looks not-happy.

"And we have to do this, why?"

"Because holidays are about generosity toward others," Dad says. "Stop whining, crew. The faster we get started, the faster we'll finish."

Soon all three of us are working together to put gifts in the bags. Each bag gets two small treats, a Slinky toy, and a book of word puzzles. I am very good and do not eat any of the candy bars. But I do grab a Slinky for myself because Slinkys are awesome.

After I finish about half the bags, I go for a Slinky break. I smile as the Slinky goes up and down, then up again.

Cookie shows up almost the moment I start playing with it. She starts pawing at the Slinky, and we turn it into a game.

"Working hard, I see," Aaron says. He's still putting candy in bags.

I know Aaron is doing that thing where people say the opposite of what they mean. It's called sarcasm. But I ignore him and smile widely.

"I sure am," I say.

That's when Cookie gets a little too excited. With a big swipe of her paw, she breaks the Slinky in half. She runs off, carrying half the Slinky in her mouth.

"I guess Cookie enjoyed her Purim gift?" I say to Dad.

"Uh-huh."

I go back to the bags.

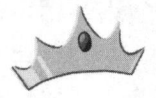

CHAPTER 14
Feelings Are Hard, Really

By the time I'm done putting stuff in the gift bags, I am *bored*. But there's still one more thing to do: Write names on all the Happy Purim cards for my class.

I sigh. Giving presents to other people is nice. I just wish that it was a little more interesting.

"Do I have to give one to Violet?" I ask Dad.

"Yes."

Making a face, I write *VIOLET* on one of the cards and tie it to a bag. I pick one that has the least-good candy bar inside it.

I write out the names of every single kid in my Hebrew school class. Soon, there's only one name left on my list: Maya.

I bite my lip. Giving a gift to Maya shouldn't feel weird at all. But it does.

Even though everything about Maya is confusing right now, I make sure to write her name in my very best handwriting. I also check the bag to make sure that she got milk chocolate because that's her favorite.

I put her bag to the side and frown.

"Why so glum?" Dad asks me.

I cross my arms over my chest. "What's *glum*?"

From across the table, Aaron smirks. He just finished up his last bag.

"*Glum*: Giving sad puppy eyes all the time. Like you."

"All right, Aaron, we don't need your help with this," Dad says.

"Cool. I've got zombies to kill!" Aaron says.

He leaves the kitchen, and within moments, I can hear the video game music coming from the living room again.

Dad turns to me.

"I'm worried about you, Rachel. I know something happened with you and Maya."

He pats me on the shoulder. "Do you want to talk about it?"

To my surprise, I do. I want to tell someone what's happening. Soon, the words are spilling out before I even have time to think about them.

"Maya is Queen Esther and not me and I got mad about that and then Maya got mad at me and we didn't talk to each other at gymnastics and then she sat with Violet at Hebrew school and I don't think we're even friends anymore!"

My voice shakes while I talk. I don't want to cry or anything. I *don't*, but I guess I am pretty glum about the whole situation.

Dad frowns. "Okay, I don't think I got everything you just said, but if I'm understanding correctly, your problems with Maya started when she got cast as Esther and you didn't. Am I right?"

I look down at the kitchen table. "Yeah."

For the longest time, Dad doesn't say anything else. And since he's not talking, I've got to say more. I need to try and explain.

"I know it's stupid," I say. "I know it's just a play and I shouldn't care so much about it."

"Rachel. Feelings aren't stupid. It's okay to care about things, and it's okay to feel disappointed that you didn't get what you wanted. But have you thought at all about how Maya must feel?"

I squirm. "I told you! She's mad at me. Like, really, really mad."

Dad nods. He still has a Serious Face up. *Gulp.*

"Yes, you said that, but think deeper. I know this is hard, but think about how you would feel if the situation were reversed.

What if you got to be Queen Esther and Maya acted not nice to you because of it?"

Well, when he puts it like that, I feel even worse about everything. I hug my arms to my chest.

"I would feel really, really hurt," I admit. "I'd think that Maya wasn't acting like a good friend."

Dad pats my shoulder again.

"Okay. I think you know what to do now."

I stare at him with my mouth open.

"Um, no? I have no idea what I should do!"

Grown-ups are the absolute weirdest sometimes. They say one thing that sounds all smart and stuff, and then they act like everything has been magically solved. But nothing has been solved!

Dad just smiles at me.

"Rachel. You weren't a good friend to

Maya, and you made her feel bad when she was happy about something. Now you need to show her that you are her friend—for real, all the time. Not just when it's fun for you."

Oh. That does make sense.

Of course, everything would be much easier if someone would explain exactly how to show Maya that I'm her friend. I want step-by-step instructions, like when we bake challah.

But Dad just says, "An apology isn't a bad way to start."

He kisses me on my head and walks away. I sigh. I think I sort of know what to do now ... but how will I know that it's going to work? What if I try my best and Maya still doesn't want to be my friend?

My face is set in a great big frown. Then I see it. Maya's Purim gift bag.

I pick my marker up again and return to

her card. Right now it just has Maya's name written on it, but that's not enough.

So I add more.

Dear Maya,
　I'm sorry.
　Can we be friends again?
　　　　　　From,
　　　　　　Rachel

I just have to hope it's good enough.

CHAPTER 15

Breaking a Leg (or Not)

Finally, the big day is here. No, not just the big day. The *ginormous* day. First, there's the Purim spiel. After that, I'm going to the Purim carnival. And through it all, I have a mission: Show Maya that I am a good friend. A fantabulous friend!

I put on my Queen Vashti dress before we leave for temple. Maybe Vashti isn't the most exciting part, but at least I get a good costume. My blue dress is the absolute prettiest, and I love it. Even though the big bow around my waist keeps coming undone. Annoying!

"Break a leg, sweetie," Dad tells me before he drops me off. All the actors have to arrive an hour before the show starts, so he's going to come back later with Aaron.

I frown. "I don't want to break a leg!"

My brother broke his leg once, and it looked really, really not-fun. I have no idea why Dad would *tell* me I should break a bone.

But Dad just laughs. "It's an expression people use in theater. I don't mean that I want you to break your leg, silly. I'm wishing you luck."

"Well, thank you very much," I say. "But I don't need luck. I've practiced every single day."

"I know, and I'm super proud of you."

That's when Dad's eyes start getting kind of watery, and I can already tell this is going to be one of those things where he acts all weird and sappy. Dads!

Luckily, we've just pulled up to the front door to the synagogue. I hop out of the car with a box full of Purim gift bags.

"See you later!" Dad calls from the window.

"See you!" I call back to him.

Of course, as I run into the building my bow starts coming undone again.

When I get to the main part of the synagogue—the sanctuary—I barely even recognize it. Normally everything is super neat. Not today. The bimah is going to be our stage, but right now it's just a mess. Props and chairs are everywhere, and I can see Ms. Rosenberg running around trying to put stuff in place.

Since there isn't anything else to do, I start handing out gift bags. Everyone likes them, even Violet. And I feel good about giving people gifts—Dad was right about that.

I save Maya's bag for last.

I find her sitting in a corner behind the bimah, wearing her Queen Esther costume. Her dress is a lot like mine, except that it's bright purple.

"You look so pretty," I blurt out when I see her.

She looks up at me, and I remember that the last time we talked things didn't exactly end well. But she nods at me.

"Thanks. You look great, too," she says.

Maybe . . . maybe she still wants to be my friend.

"I guess we're both queens," I say. "That's pretty cool."

"Mm-hmm."

I bite my lip. This isn't exactly going the way I'd hoped... but at least Maya isn't telling me to go away. That must mean something, right?

"I got you a gift bag for Purim," I say. "I mean, I made gift bags for everyone. But yours has milk chocolate."

I hand the bag to her. She takes it and smiles.

"Thanks, Rachel."

Well. It's a start.

I just hope she likes my note.

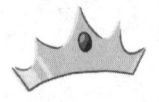

CHAPTER 16

The Purim Spiel

Once I'm done talking to Maya, I start playing with the Slinky I brought with me. I'm nervous—just a little bit!—and the Slinky helps calm me down.

"Three minutes until showtime!" Ms. Rosenberg calls out finally. She is using her very biggest in-charge voice. "Get ready to go onstage, please."

I stop playing with the Slinky. It's time.

I want to be extra sure that I'm ready for the big moment, so I rush toward the bimah. I don't notice until too late that the bow around my waist has gotten untied. Or that I've accidentally stepped on it. The whole bow is completely torn off.

"Oh no," I whisper. "Oh no, no, no."

I pick up the rumpled ribbon. I stare at it. I know it doesn't really matter. It's just a costume. But . . . before, I really did look like a queen. Now everything is just *wrong*.

Don't cry, I tell myself. I can't cry right before the play starts! But my eyes prickle anyway.

"Rachel? Do you need help?"

I spin around to face Maya standing a few feet away. She's looking at me with a frown. Not an angry frown, though. More like an I-care-about-you frown.

I swallow hard. "Yes. Please. Help would be very, very good."

Maya takes the ribbon from me. She ties it around my waist twice and then starts on a knot. The ribbon feels nice and tight on me. Then, like magic, Maya ties the ribbon into a beautiful bow.

"My mama taught me how to make a special knot," Maya says. "That should stay put for the whole show."

I break into a smile so big it almost makes my cheeks hurt.

"Oh my gosh, Maya, thank you, thank you, thank you! You just saved my life, and also the entire show."

Maya smiles back at me. "I don't know about that. But, um, you're welcome?"

I want to tell her thank you again. I want to ask if she saw my note. I want to ask if we're back to being friends. But before I can, Ms. Rosenberg is yelling out instructions.

"Places!" she calls.

The show is about to begin.

I may not have many lines in the play. But I do a stupendous job with every single one of them. If I do say so myself.

"I'd rather give up my crown than listen to you!" I tell Ben, also known as King Long-Name.

"Fine, then!" Ben says back.

With that, I exit the stage. I'll be watching the rest of the show from the side of the bimah.

I look over at Maya. As she's getting ready to go on, she chews on her bottom lip. I know what that means: She's nervous.

"You're going to be great," I tell her.

Maya doesn't look so sure about that. "I hope so."

I want to say more. But she needs to go on soon, and there's no time for talking.

"... and Mordechai had a beautiful cousin named Esther," Violet says from the edge of the bimah.

Maya walks toward the center of the stage, looking just like Queen Esther. I mean, I don't actually know what Queen Esther looked like, but I'm sure she was like Maya: pretty and super sweet.

It's time for Maya's first line. I know what it is, and so does she. I've heard her say it five million times in rehearsals.

Only ... now Maya doesn't say a word. She opens her mouth, then closes it. She looks totally panicked, and for a second, I'm worried we're going to have a repeat of the throwing-up-before-the-gymnastics-meet thing.

Well, I'm here to help. In my place on the side of the stage, I wave my arms at her like a giant bird, trying to get her attention. I think it works. Then, I loudly whisper the line: "Cousin Mordechai, do you really think I can be the queen?"

Maya blinks. Then she repeats the line.

She doesn't forget a single word for the rest of the play.

When we take a bow at the end of the show, Maya grips my hand tightly.

CHAPTER 17
The Meaning of Purim

As soon as the play is over, Maya and I both start talking.

"I'm sorry about everything!" I say. "I am soooo sorry."

"Thank you, thank you, thank you," she says at the same time.

"Maybe you should go first," I suggest.

Maya grins.

"You saved me back there."

"You did most of that yourself. But I'm glad to help," I tell her. "We're *friends*."

For a moment, neither one of us says anything else. I try to gather my thoughts. This is super important, and I need to get it right.

"I'm really sorry about how I've been acting," I say at last. "I was a real jerk to you because I was jealous."

Maya looks down.

"I was so happy about being Esther, and I was expecting you to be happy for me, too. Because you're my best friend! But then it was like you were mad at me because of it."

My skin starts to feel prickly and uncomfortable.

"I know. I should have been happy for you, even though I also felt bad for me."

Looking up at me, Maya nods. Her body relaxes.

"It's okay for you to feel sad for yourself. But it felt like you were taking your bad feelings out on me."

She's right. I'm supposed to be Maya's friend—her *very bestest friend in the entire universe* —but I didn't act like it. I was too busy moping.

"I know. I should have cared more about your feelings, not just mine."

"And it's like . . . everything was already so hard!" Maya says. "Being Esther made me super nervous. Plus, so many people already think I'm not even Jewish because I'm Black! And then you were mad at me . . ."

I play with my hands as I think. Maya needs me to be a good friend right now. I need to say the right things.

"I don't think that at all," I tell her.

"I know, but the way you acted made me feel like you thought you deserved to be Esther and I didn't."

"I'm sorry. I didn't even think about that, but I should have," I say. "I need to do better at thinking about your feelings."

I look at Maya, and she looks at me.

"I missed you," she says.

"I missed you, too!"

Another too-long silence. I decide to break it.

"So . . . so does this mean we're friends again?"

Maya grins at me. "Yes. I want to be friends again."

I feel like doing a cartwheel in celebration. Although that's probably a bad idea with my costume.

"So I guess Violet isn't your new best friend?" I ask.

"Are you kidding?" Maya asks. She shakes her head. "She's not my friend at all! I'm so tired of hearing about her new dress from Paris."

I grin.

"Let's do our special handshake," I say.

And we do.

Lucky for us, Purim isn't over just yet. We still have one of the very best parts: the Purim carnival!

The big room next to the sanctuary has been completely changed into a carnival. Everywhere I look, there's another game or art project to try. Right away, I'm excited about Hit the Hamantaschen, Pin the Crown on Esther, and Make a Grager.

"What do you want to do, Rachel?" Maya asks.

"Everything!" I say. "But you can pick first."

We start with Hit the Hamantaschen. Maya starts throwing beanbags into a giant, painted hamantaschen. While she focuses on the game, I look around the room. The entire synagogue must be here!

And everyone, everywhere, is wearing a costume.

I see Ms. Rosenberg a few feet away by the Wheel of Purim game. She's wearing a jester hat, and her face is painted like a clown. A pretty clown, not a creepy clown. I run up to her so I can say hi.

"Hi, Ms. Rosenberg!"

She smiles at me in that teacher way, which is kind of weird coming from a clown.

"Hello, Rachel. You did a wonderful job today!"

I bite my lip. I still have a big, big question for her. But if my dad were here he'd tell me to say thank you, so that's what I do.

"Can I ask you a question?" I say after I'm done showing my manners.

"Of course!" Ms. Rosenberg responds.

This is it. This is my chance.

"Why did you give me the part of Queen Vashti? I mean, it's not very important."

Ms. Rosenberg frowns.

"Rachel, every part is important."

"I know, but . . ."

I trail off. I'm not sure how to say what I want to say.

"I'm not sure you do know," Ms. Rosenberg tells me. "Rachel, do you know what the meaning of Purim is?"

Well, I wasn't expecting her to ask a question like *that*. Now that she mentions it, what *is* the meaning of Purim? I have a lot of ideas, but I'm not sure any of them are right. But I try anyway.

"I guess the meaning of Purim is that Haman was really bad, and we should boo him?" I guess. "And also that dressing up in costumes is fun, and we should give gifts to people."

My teacher smiles at me.

"Those are all good answers. Do you want to know what I think the meaning of Purim is?"

"Yeah?"

"For me, the meaning of Purim is the same as most other Jewish holidays. It's about celebrating our Jewish community."

"Oh," I say.

That's definitely smarter than "costumes are fun." I guess that's why she's a teacher.

"I know it was disappointing for you to not get the biggest part," Ms. Rosenberg says. "But Purim isn't about one person. Not even Queen Esther herself. Purim is about all of us, together. Does that make sense?"

"I think so?" I say, even though I'm still not 100 percent sure.

"Let's put it this way. Do you think you did a good job as Vashti?"

"Yes!"

"And do you think Maya did a good job as Esther?"

"Of course she did!"

Ms. Rosenberg smiles at me. "Then I think it's clear that you both did a great job for our class and our community. That's what matters."

"I guess . . . I guess that makes sense," I say.

"I'm glad you think so," Ms. Rosenberg tells me. "Maybe next time we do a play, you will have more lines. I know you can handle it. But today, I think you should be very, very proud of yourself."

Now I think I understand what Ms. Rosenberg is saying.

I look back over at Maya. She punches her fist in the air, so she must have won the game. Yay for her!

"Okay," I say to Ms. Rosenberg. "Thank you for telling me smart teacher stuff."

She laughs. "Any time."

I give her a thumbs-up before I go back to the game and back to my best friend.

Maya pats me on the shoulder.

"Your turn, Rachel!"

Acknowledgments

Just as Purim is a community holiday, so too is writing and publishing a book. I could not have written this third part of Rachel's story without support from an entire team. First, thank you to my editor, Dana Chidiac. Your comments always offer a clear roadmap of what I need to do. I would also like to extend a huge thanks to the entire team at Macmillan: Ann Marie Wong, Jean Feiwel, Valery Badio, Alexei Esikoff, Sarah Gompper, Abby Granata,

Aurora Parlagreco, Molly Ellis, Mary Van Akin, Mariel Dawson, Chantal Gersch, and Shawn Foster.

As always, a huge thanks to my agent, Jennifer Laughran, her assistant Bex Livermore, and the entire team at Andrea Brown Literary Agency.

Genevieve Kote deserves an extra-special thank-you for creating another beautiful set of illustrations that perfectly capture Rachel and her world. I smile widely every time Genevieve's art appears in my inbox, and I know that readers will love her work just as much as I do.

Thank you to the entire team at Recorded Books for transforming Rachel's stories into audiobooks.

Thanks muchly to Neil and the rest of my family, for your unwavering support. A special thanks to my sister Elli for spreading the word about my books to Jewish educators.

And, last but not least, thank you to all of the readers, teachers, and librarians who have read and shared Rachel's stories. You make all of the challenges worthwhile.